For Grandmas and Grandads everywhere,
and for all their grandchildren.

Special thanks to Kristina Petersen for her multilingual Santa mail, and to Mum for last-minute proofreading.

Text and illustrations copyright © 2021 by Chris Naylor-Ballesteros

Tundra Books, an imprint of Penguin Random House Canada Young Readers, a division of Penguin Random House of Canada Limited

First published in Great Britain in 2021 by Andersen Press Ltd.

Library and Archives Canada Cataloguing in Publication available upon request

ISBN 9780735271180 (hardcover) ISBN 9780735271197 (epub)

Published simultaneously in the United States of America by Tundra Books of Northern New York, an imprint of Penguin Random House Canada Young Readers, a division of Penguin Random House of Canada Limited

Library of Congress Control Number: 2020948998

Printed in China

www.penguinrandomhouse.ca

1   2   3   4   5   25   24   23   22   21

Tiny Reindeer

Chris Naylor-Ballesteros

tundra

Tiny Reindeer was just like any other reindeer, but with one big difference. He was very, very tiny.
He wasn't just smaller than the others, he felt different too.
And never more so than at one particular time of year . . .

Christmas time.

As Christmas came ever nearer, the big, stamping, snorting reindeer were busy helping Santa get ready for the most important night of the year.

"Ho! Ho! Ho! Let's get to it, there are jobs to be done!" boomed Santa, as he fed his herd.

"Ho . . . ho . . . humph," sighed Tiny Reindeer. "I wish there was a job I could do, even just a *tiny* one."

Every year Tiny Reindeer tried
very hard to find a way to help,
but whatever he did went wrong.
He got tangled in the reins
and harnesses.

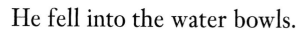

He fell into the water bowls.

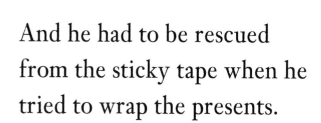

And he had to be rescued
from the sticky tape when he
tried to wrap the presents.

On the day before Christmas Eve, Santa spoke to Tiny Reindeer. "Why don't you have a look in the Mail Room? You might be able to help there," he suggested, kindly. "There's one last little pile of children's letters to sort."
Tiny Reindeer wasn't so sure.

A *little* pile? Tiny ended up squashed under an enormous mess of mixed-up Christmas letters. But as he struggled to wriggle free, a letter with a reindeer drawn on it caught his eye. It was from a little girl. "Hmm. Maybe this one's for me," he thought.

Against all the rules, Tiny sneaked it away with him to his quiet little corner of the stables and read it. And he came up with a plan.

The next morning everyone was busy getting ready for takeoff. And as nighttime fell, Santa took the reins of his magnificent sleigh, harnessing the puffing reindeer for the long journey ahead.

Nobody noticed a tiny
passenger leaping into a hiding place
on the back of Santa's sleigh — a secret voyager on a special mission.

Throughout the long and snowy night, Santa's sleigh flew across the sky, crossing oceans and covering continents.

Tiny Reindeer stayed hidden until, finally, the moment he'd waited for had arrived.

He took a deep breath and leapt from the sleigh into the freezing air as Santa and his galloping herd disappeared into the darkness.

From a bag on Tiny Reindeer's back ballooned
a perfectly sized paper parachute made from
the little girl's letter. He aimed for the chimney of
one particular house, and . . .

Whoosh . . .

He plunged through the hole, tumbling into the fireplace below.

After climbing out, he tiptoed towards an open door,

which led to a hallway   and an enormous staircase.

"Oh no," thought Tiny Reindeer. The stairs were far too big for him. Tired and cold, he couldn't climb the first one, let alone all the others. And he didn't even know if he had landed in the right house. As he lowered his head and tears came to his eyes, Tiny Reindeer began to wonder if he'd made a very big mistake.

Suddenly there was a noise in the room behind him, a crash and a bash, a huffing and a puffing, then footsteps moving across the floor. Tiny Reindeer tried to hide in the shadows, keeping quiet and still.

But a huge figure stepped into the hallway and looked straight down at him . . .

Santa!

"Good thing I was keeping an eye on you, Tiny Reindeer," he whispered. "It looks like you could do with some help."

Santa carefully took off the paper parachute and folded it into his coat pocket. Then, dusting off the soot and dirt, he carried Tiny Reindeer upstairs to a bedroom where a little girl was fast asleep. A beautiful, tiny wooden sleigh sat right beside her.

She didn't hear the door open, nor did she see Santa tiptoe across the floor. She didn't even stir when Tiny Reindeer leapt softly onto her pillow.

"Goodbye, my little friend. I must be on my way," Santa whispered. "I'll try to drop in and see you next year."

And then he was gone.

Tiny Reindeer settled down, warm and cozy on the pillow. Exhausted after his adventure, he wondered what Christmas morning might bring, until eventually he yawned and closed his eyes.

The little girl remained fast asleep, dreaming excitedly of a tiny sleigh and . . .

"A tiny reindeer! *My* tiny reindeer!" she cried out when she woke on Christmas morning. Tiny stood proudly on the little girl's hands and knew he had finally found where he belonged — and with the most beautiful sleigh he'd ever seen, handmade to fit him perfectly.

His plan had worked . . .

with just a tiny bit of help from Santa.